My
Adorable
Pony

For Lorna and Alison Hawkins – who are both my sisters and my best friends. S.H.

Scholastic Children's Books
An imprint of Scholastic Ltd
Euston House, 24 Eversholt Street, London, NW1 1DB, UK
Registered office: Westfield Road, Southam, Warwickshire, CV47 0RA
SCHOLASTIC and associated logos are trademarks and/or
registered trademarks of Scholastic Inc.

First published in the UK by Scholastic Ltd, 2016

Text copyright © Scholastic Ltd, 2016

ISBN 978 1407 16250 8

A CIP catalogue record for this book
is available from the British Library.

All rights reserved.
This book is sold subject to the condition that it shall not,
by way of trade or otherwise, be lent, hired out or otherwise circulated in
any form of binding or cover other than that in which it is published. No
part of this publication may be reproduced, stored in a retrieval system,
or transmitted in any form or by any means (electronic, mechanical,
photocopying, recording or otherwise) without prior
written permission of Scholastic Limited.

Printed by CPI Group (UK) Ltd, Croydon, CR0 4YY
Papers used by Scholastic Children's Books are made
from wood grown in sustainable forests.

1 3 5 7 9 10 8 6 4 2

This is a work of fiction. Names, characters, places, incidents
and dialogues are products of the author's imagination or are used
fictitiously. Any resemblance to actual people, living or dead,
events or locales is entirely coincidental.

www.scholastic.co.uk

My
Adorable
Pony

Sarah Hawkins

SCHOLASTIC

1

Clara looked out of the car window excitedly as they drove down the country lane. "We're here!" Mum called out.

"Where?" Clara leaned forward in her seat and peered outside. "Where are we?" Mum and Dad had been so mysterious about their day trip. They wouldn't tell her where they were going, but just said that they were taking her for a surprise. Clara was desperate to find out what it was!

As Dad slowed down, they drove past a big sign. "Hollyhock Stables," Clara read out loud, then gasped. Stables meant one thing – ponies! Clara loved ponies. She had been horse-mad ever since she could remember. She loved the way they looked, their long, beautiful manes and their kind eyes. She'd read lots of books about unicorns, but to Clara, horses and ponies seemed just as magical. *But what were they doing at a stable?* "Are we going to see some horses?" she asked. Then she had a brilliant thought and squealed in excitement. "Am I going to have a riding lesson? That would be AMAZING!"

"Hold your horses!" Dad joked as he parked the car.

Mum turned around in the front seat. "You know how you've asked for a pony for every birthday and Christmas present since you were little?" she said with a grin.

Clara nodded, twirling her finger in her long brown hair.

"Well, Daddy and I got a bit of extra money recently," Mum said. "And we thought we could have a nice holiday, or a new car … or we could spend it giving you what you want most in the world."

"You're getting a pony!" Dad said, with a massive grin. "Or a horse. Whichever one is smaller."

"A pony," Clara told him automatically. Then she realized what he'd said. "I'm getting a pony?" she squealed. She glanced from Mum to Dad and they both nodded. Clara didn't know what to say. This surprise was better than she could ever have imagined! "Thank you! Thank you SO MUCH!" she shrieked.

Mum opened the car door and Clara burst out to hug her. Then she ran round the other side to give Dad a squeeze too.

Mum laughed. "Come on, a lady's waiting to show us some ponies!"

With Mum and Dad following behind, Clara skipped through the gate and up to a big yard surrounded by stalls and, beyond them, fields. In one field, she could see a big, patchy black-and-white horse and a smaller grey pony. They were galloping around, their manes streaming out behind them. Clara stopped to watch. She was grinning so much that her cheeks ached. She couldn't believe that she was getting a pony of her own!

As they walked across the yard, a line of horses and ponies poked their heads over their stall doors, looking at Clara curiously as she passed. Clara felt her heart beating faster – one of them could be hers!

"Mr and Mrs Walker?" A lady was hurrying across the yard to meet them, wiping her hands on her jodhpurs. She was tall, and her red hair was tied up in a messy bun with bits of straw sticking out of it. She was wearing a navy jumper with a galloping white horse logo and "Hollyhock

Stables" stitched on to it. "I'm Sally Archer, the stable owner."

"I'm George. This is Lizzie – and our daughter, Clara," Dad said.

Sally looked at Clara. Her brown eyes crinkled as she smiled. "My daughter Milly's about your age." She pointed over to a field where a girl was riding a grey pony around a series of jumps, watched by a stable hand. Wild, curly red hair was sticking out from underneath her helmet. As they watched, the girl leant forward and the pony leapt gracefully over one jump, then the next. Clara felt like clapping. *Maybe one day I'll be able to do that!* she thought to herself.

Clara jumped as Dad put his hand on her shoulder. "Clara is the reason we're here," he explained. "As I said on the phone, we need a pony who's going to be safe for a beginner."

"Absolutely," Sally nodded. "I have the

perfect one." She grinned at Clara. "Do you want to meet Honey?"

Clara nodded wordlessly. Honey was such a pretty name! She and her best friend, Lisa, had always talked about what they'd call their pony if they were lucky enough to get one, but they hadn't thought of anything as nice as Honey! Clara couldn't help feeling a tiny bit pleased that she was getting a pony before Lisa. Her friend normally had everything first.

Sally led them through the riding school, pointing things out as they went. "There's the tack room and the feed room. We have lots of fields, and both an indoor and outdoor school..."

Clara was only half listening; she was too busy looking at every pony they passed, wondering if it was Honey. But Sally kept on going until they reached the stall at the very end.

Inside was the most beautiful horse Clara had ever seen! The sunshine was glinting off her chestnut-coloured coat. She had a dark chocolate-brown mane and tail, the same colour as Clara's hair. As they got closer, Honey shuffled her hooves and turned to look at them. Clara saw that she had four white fetlocks – like little socks on her feet – and a white blaze down the middle of her nose. She was gorgeous!

"Her full name is Honey Rose Duchess," Sally explained. "And she's just as sweet as honey! She's eight years old and thirteen hands high, and she's really kind and patient, perfect for a beginner. Her last owner got too tall to ride her, otherwise they would have kept her."

Honey whickered curiously as she looked at them. The happy horse noise sent a thrill through Clara. "Can I stroke her?" she asked.

"Of course," Sally smiled.

Clara stepped into the stall, reaching up to touch the white blaze on Honey's nose. Honey smelled her hand, then let herself be stroked. Her nose was warm and velvety soft. Clara had to try really hard not to squeal out loud. She was stroking her very own pony!

"Here, give her one of these and she'll be your friend for life." Sally reached into her pocket and brought out a packet of Polo mints. She tipped one into Clara's hand, and Honey shifted her hooves excitedly.

"Keep your hand flat," Sally instructed.

Clara held out the Polo and gasped as Honey brought her head close to her shoulder and huffed softly. Her breath was warm and sweet, and Clara giggled as it blew her fringe away from her face. "Go on, it's OK," she said gently, offering Honey the Polo. Honey stared at her with deep brown eyes, blinked happily, then took the treat from her hand.

Clara had a sudden thought. "Where would she live?" she asked, turning to her parents.

"Well, we're not taking her home and putting her in the back garden!" Mum joked. "We'd keep her in livery, so she'd live here and be looked after. The riding school will exercise her on the days you aren't able to. You could come for riding lessons twice a week to start with, and we'll see how we go."

"We've got a team of grooms who'll take good care of her," Sally said.

Clara stroked Honey's neck while Sally got Honey to lift her feet for Mum and Dad to inspect. Mum and Dad didn't know anything about horses, but Dad was nodding as Sally showed Honey off.

While the adults talked, Clara kept stroking Honey's soft nose. Honey put her head down and gently nudged Clara's shoulder.

"What do you think, darling?" Dad asked in a serious tone. "You don't have to pick Honey. We can keep looking and choose whichever pony you like the best."

Clara couldn't believe Dad was even asking. "Dad! Honey's perfect!" She gave a little squeal. "I can't believe she could be mine!"

"What do you think, Honey?" Sally asked, reaching a hand out to stroke the pony.

Clara found herself holding her breath as she looked at Honey. Then, with a happy whicker, Honey nodded her head.

The adults laughed as if it was a coincidence, but Clara knew – she hadn't chosen Honey; they'd chosen each other!

Clara was curled up in her pyjamas on the sofa with her mum, watching a TV programme on whales. She could feel herself yawning and tried her best to hide it. It was nearly ten o'clock, but she was determined to stay up until Dad got home. She'd had the most amazing riding lesson and she wanted to tell him all about it! Clara had been riding Honey for three months now, and she was getting better every lesson. She now knew how to walk, do a rising trot and canter. Best of all, Honey seemed to love their lessons as much as she did.

"I think you'd better go to bed, darling," Mum said as the whale programme finished. "It's way past bedtime."

"But Dad's not back from work yet, and I want to tell him about Honey. Please can I stay up?" Clara begged. "Please! Please!" She knelt on the sofa and wrapped her arms around Mum's neck.

Mum pulled her into a hug and gave her a kiss on the forehead. "Hmmmm," she said. "It *is* Friday night... But as soon as he's home, off to bed and no arguments. OK?"

"OK!" Clara agreed happily.

"Maybe we can have some secret ice cream since Dad's not around?" Mum suggested with a naughty grin.

Just then they heard the car door slam outside. Mum rolled her eyes. "Perfect timing!"

Clara giggled and ran to open the front door.

"There's my darling girl!" Dad declared as he walked into the lounge.

"Hi, Daddy!" Clara jumped up and buried her face in his suit, giving him a big hug.

Dad dropped a kiss on the top of Clara's head. "I've got something for you. Close your eyes and put out your hands."

Clara squealed with delight. A present!

She shut her eyes and held out her palms. Dad put something into them, and when she opened her eyes, she saw it was a box wrapped in brightly coloured paper. "Go on, open it," Dad said.

Clara tore open the wrapping paper. Inside the box was a new riding helmet! The hard exterior was black and shining, but the lining was silky pink. "Look, Mum!" she said with a grin.

"It's very nice, darling, but I'm not sure you need it," Mum said. She frowned at Dad. "You've only had your old one for a few months."

"Do you like it?" Dad asked.

"Yes, thank you!" Clara reached up on tiptoe to give him a kiss on his cheek.

"Right then, off to bed," Dad said.

"But you just got home!" Clara complained.

"Daddy will be here all weekend," Mum said.

Dad shrugged off his jacket with a sigh. "Actually I do have to go into the office tomorrow. But we'll have lots of time together, I promise."

"She's got her riding lesson tomorrow, remember," Mum said, looking cross. "We said we'd go and watch because they're starting to learn something new."

"Oh, yes!" Clara grinned. "Guess what?"

"Um, you got elected as Prime Minister?" Dad teased.

"No!" Clara said. "Don't be silly. It's about me and Honey."

"You won the pony Olympics?" Dad guessed, pulling a funny face.

"No! We're going to learn how to jump!" Clara told him. "It's our first lesson tomorrow, and then in the summer the whole stable is going to have a gymkhana – which is a day of special horse races and games – and our class is going to do jumping in front of everyone!"

Clara couldn't wait to start jumping. She loved the thought of being on Honey's back as she leapt through the air – it would be like flying!

"We'll be there," Mum said. She turned to Dad and raised an eyebrow. "Won't we?"

"Of course," Dad promised. "Now, bedtime."

Clara gave them both a hug and went out of the lounge. The door had barely closed behind her when she heard them start arguing, their voices overlapping with each other in fierce, angry murmurings. She went upstairs and got into bed, trying not to listen to the muffled voices below. Mum and Dad were always fighting now, and it made her feel cold and shivery inside. She twisted her hair around her finger and tried to think about something nice. Immediately she thought about riding Honey, with her best friend Lisa riding next to her. Lisa had got her own pony, a big bay mare called Star, soon after Clara had got Honey. They both kept them at the riding school, and went there as often as they could.

As a door slammed downstairs. Clara grabbed her pillow and thought about jumping on Honey and cantering away, her hair and Honey's mane flying in the wind. With a smile, Clara fell fast asleep.

2

It was early when Mum and Clara arrived at the stables the next morning, but it was already hot and sunny. Clara was dressed in her riding clothes – black jodhpur leggings, a pink top and brown boots – and she was carrying her new riding hat. Mum had made her put suntan cream on her face and arms.

"Daddy will be here as soon as he finishes his work," said Mum, and she gave her a kiss for luck.

Clara nodded. The butterflies in her tummy were fluttering around. She always felt a funny mix of calm and excited when she got to the stables and breathed in the familiar scent of hay and horses. She ran over to the tack room, where Sally, their riding teacher, had told the class to meet.

The five other girls in her class were already waiting there. "Clara!" Lisa cried, coming over to give her a hug. She was dressed in fancy riding clothes and her short blonde hair was neatly tied back in a stubby French plait. "Is that a new helmet? My old one was just like that!"

Before Clara could reply, Sally clapped her hands. "Right, girls – as you know, today we're going to start learning how to jump." She brought out a pile of thick body warmers. "These are body protectors. You're all good riders, but there's still a chance you could fall, and these will keep you in one piece if you do. I know it's hot, but we have to be safe. Grab one and let's go – the horses are all ready."

Three of the grooms were holding the horses just outside the indoor riding school. Clara's heart jumped as she saw Honey standing next to Star. She grabbed a body protector and raced over to take the reins from the groom who was holding her.

"Hi, Honey!" Clara grinned. She gave Honey a stroke and her pony whickered in delight.

"I missed you too," Clara whispered as she put her forehead against Honey's smooth cheek. "Are you ready to do some jumping?"

As Clara rode Honey into the indoor school, she looked out for Mum and Dad. Mum was sitting, waving, in the fenced-off viewing area. Next to her, her bag was saving a seat. *Where's Dad?* Clara wondered. She tried to wave to Mum, but just then Honey shook her head and Clara had to reach down to pat her. She needed to concentrate if they were going to learn how to jump!

"Right, to begin with we're going to warm up the ponies with some trotting around the edge of the circuit," Sally called out as the girls began to walk in a circle around the inside of the school. "Sit deep, elbows back, shoulders back, and get ready to t . . . rot!"

Clara leaned forwards a little, keeping her hands soft on the reins as they moved into a trot. She and Honey were at the front of the line, with the other girls and their ponies trotting behind her. She felt a thrill of excitement as she saw a line of poles on the floor in the middle of the barn.

The light was streaming through the high windows. Clara could smell the sawdust on the floor, and hear the clopping of hooves and the huff of the horses' breath as they exercised. Honey was warm beneath her, her chestnut coat shining in the sunshine, and from the tilt of her head and the flicking of her ears, Clara could tell she was excited.

Once they'd trotted around the edge of the arena a few times, Sally got them to line up in a row. This time, Clara was last, behind all the others. As they waited, she patted Honey's side. Sally called Lisa and Star to go first. Lisa trotted her horse once around the circuit, then went slowly up to the poles. As Star stepped neatly over one pole then another, Clara twiddled her hair nervously. Pari was next, with her white gelding, Misty. They didn't do quite as well. Pari didn't turn Misty quickly enough, so they missed two of the poles in the middle. "Good start," Sally said. "Next time make sure you point him where you want him to go."

One by one, the other girls in the class

took their turns, until just Clara and Honey were left. Finally Sally turned to them. "OK, Clara, your go!"

"Come on, Honey!" Clara squeezed Honey's flanks with her knees to make her trot forward. But when they got to the first pole, Honey refused to go over it. She tossed her head and stepped to one side, trotting around it instead.

Clara straightened up so that they were directly in front of the next pole, but Honey did the same thing again. Clara leaned low over Honey's neck. "What's up?" she asked, stroking her reassuringly.

"Never mind," Sally called cheerfully. "Try again."

But no matter what Clara did, Honey wouldn't walk over the poles. Clara glanced across at the seats and saw Mum watching anxiously.

Sally came over to check that they were

22

all right. She took the reins and led Honey towards the first pole, but as soon as her hooves got near it, Honey shied away, stepping back awkwardly and shaking her head from side to side.

Sally soothed her. "OK, we're going to have to take it slowly with Honey," she told Clara. "I don't know why, she's not green..."

Clara's face must have looked confused, because Sally smiled. "'Green' is what we call horses that have never been trained," she explained. "Honey has done all this before, but maybe she has some bad memories of jumping. Maybe her last owner overfaced her – tried to make her jump something that was too big – and it scared her. Horses are very good at remembering things they didn't like. We're going to have to show her that jumping is fun."

Clara reached over and stroked Honey's neck. "It's OK," she murmured.

Honey's ears were flickering nervously to and fro, and they didn't stop until they were away from the poles. Across the barn, Clara could see Lisa talking to the other girls, her face flushed and happy. Clara was disappointed that she and Honey weren't doing better, but most of all she was worried about Honey.

"Right, that's enough for today," Sally cried out. "Everyone, do a few more circuits and then we'll give the horses a rub down."

"Come on, Honey." Clara kicked her heels and turned Honey towards the barn door.

As they went past the viewing area, she glanced over at her mum. Mum waved and gave her a shrug as if to say "You'll do better next time". But Clara couldn't stop staring at the empty seat next to her. Dad hadn't come.

24

"I did the poles three times!" Lisa said as she and Clara trotted their horses into the yard. "What do you think is wrong with Honey?"

Clara just shrugged. She was deep in thought as she led Honey over to the mounting block and got down.

"She'll learn," Lisa said airily, as if she knew all about jumping and it wasn't her first lesson too. "Oh, I almost forgot – Mum's invited you over to our house after we finish."

"Thanks," Clara said distractedly. She hoped Honey was OK. Now that they were away from the poles, she seemed to be back to her usual self. Her ears had pricked up and her breathing was back to normal.

"Milly, can you come and help with untacking and rubbing down?" Sally called to her daughter.

Milly ran over. She and Clara smiled

at each other. Clara always remembered seeing Milly jumping the first time she came to the stables. She was so good that even though they were the same age, Milly was in the advanced classes. Milly and her mum had a house in the stables, so she was always around. Clara wished she could spend all her time with the horses like Milly did!

"Come on, let's go!" Lisa said. She got off Star and gave Milly the reins, heading towards her mum without giving Star another glance. Milly led Star into her stable, stroking the bay mare's mane and murmuring to her.

"In a minute!" Clara called. She wished they didn't have to leave straight away. Lisa did violin and ice-skating lessons as well as horse riding, and sometimes Clara wondered which she liked best. Riding Honey was Clara's favourite thing in the whole world, but for Lisa it seemed like it was just one of many activities.

Clara kissed Honey on her nose. Honey whickered in delight and nuzzled into her. Clara knew what she wanted. "Here you go, girl." She gave her a Polo. "See you next week," she whispered.

"Come on, Clara!" Lisa called from across the yard.

Clara gave Honey one more pat and sped off towards the others. She didn't turn back, but she felt sure that Honey was staring sadly after her.

U

Clara had a brilliant time at Lisa's house. They played in her swimming pool, splashing and pretending to be mermaids. It was so nice to be out of the hot body protector and her sticky riding hat.

"Lisa, why don't you tell Clara about your

summer camp," Lisa's mum called from the kitchen, where she and Clara's mum were having a cup of tea.

"Come up to my room!" Lisa said.

They ran upstairs with towels wrapped around their swimming costumes, their hair still dripping wet. Lisa grabbed her iPad and brought something up on the screen.

"Rosendale Summer Camp," Clara read out loud. The picture on the screen was of a group of kids riding ponies though a dappled forest. Lisa flicked the screen and there was another showing riders galloping along a beach. It looked amazing!

"I'm going for six whole weeks!" Lisa shrieked. "You have to ask your parents if you can come with me! It's going to be AMAZING!"

Clara grinned as Lisa showed her pictures of wooden huts full of bunk beds, stables and a huge dining hall where everyone ate.

"How does Star get there?" she asked.

"Oh, she's not coming," Lisa replied, rubbing her hair with the towel. "You can't take your own pony; you have to use one of theirs. But they're all amazing ponies." She showed Clara a page with pictures of beautiful ponies and a description of them underneath. "I hope I get Peppermint," Lisa said dreamily. "He used to be owned by a real-life princess!"

Clara made *ooh*ing and *ahh*ing noises as they looked at the ponies, but secretly she thought that none of them looked as nice as Honey and Star. Lisa flicked back through the pictures, and Clara stared at the one of the girl cantering her horse along the beach. She had a picture just like that in her bedroom. She'd always wanted to ride on the beach, but whenever she'd imagined it, it had been Honey she was riding. It wouldn't be as good if she couldn't share it with her.

"You *have* to come," Lisa said.

"I don't know..." Clara replied.

"Please!" Lisa said enthusiastically. "We could share a bunk bed. It would be brilliant!"

"I wouldn't see Honey for six whole weeks," Clara mumbled. "I haven't spent that long away from her since I got her. And what about the gymkhana?"

"I'll miss Star too," Lisa said, her blue eyes wide. "But they'll still be here when we get back. We'll learn to jump at camp, and then we'll be the best riders at the gymkhana. What's better – having a boring old summer here, or riding every day at Pony Camp!"

"Pony Camp!" Clara said with a laugh.

"Yay!" Lisa flung her arms around her and gave her a soggy hug.

"I haven't asked my parents yet!" Clara said.

"They'll say yes!" Lisa said as they ran back outside.

Clara laughed as she followed her friend. "We're going to Pony Camp!" they squealed, laughing and dancing around.

3

Clara and Lisa spent the next week whispering at school about Pony Camp. Clara still hadn't asked her parents if she could go. They'd been arguing even more recently, and most nights Dad hadn't been home from work before Clara went to bed. Lisa's parents had already booked her place at Pony Camp, and Lisa wanted Clara to get hers too before they all sold out. By Friday, Clara was determined to ask her parents, then she and Lisa could talk about it at their riding lesson tomorrow.

Mum was quiet as they drove home from school, but Clara was pleased to see Dad's car in the driveway when they arrived back at the house. She raced indoors to get changed out of her school uniform, but to her surprise, Dad called her into the lounge.

"Clara, darling, can you come in here a minute?" he said.

Mum followed her in and sat on the sofa, twisting a tissue in her hands. She patted the seat next to her and Clara sat down, a cold, nervous feeling suddenly appearing in the pit of her stomach.

"We've got some news," Dad said gently. "And I think it's going to be a shock, so you have to be very brave, OK?"

Clara nodded, her fingers fiddling nervously with her hair.

"I'm afraid that Mummy and I are going to be getting a divorce," Dad said solemnly.

Clara stared at her parents.

"We both love you very, very much," Mum said, putting her arm around Clara's shoulders. "And that's never, ever going to change. But Daddy and I both think we'd be happier if we didn't live together any more."

Mum looked at her with tears in her eyes. Clara looked from her to Dad, then down at her shoes. Lots of her friends' parents were divorced, but somehow, even with all the fighting, she didn't think it would happen to her parents. Mum and Dad were both looking at her like they wanted her to say something. "Oh," she said, in a small voice.

"Daddy's going to move out for now," Mum explained. "And then we'll both find new houses. You can help us choose!"

"We're moving?" Clara gasped. Somehow that was an even bigger shock. She didn't want to move house. She wanted to live here, where she'd always lived, with both Mum and Dad, and for nothing to change.

"I'm so sorry, darling," Mum said. "But it'll be OK, I promise."

She tried to give Clara a hug, but Clara wriggled away. She ran upstairs to her room. Below her, she could hear Mum and Dad's voices as they started to argue again.

U

Clara's eyes felt puffy and gritty when she woke up. For a second she wondered why. Then she remembered about her parents. She looked around her bedroom. It had been the same ever since she was a baby, with its light-pink walls and white curtains with pink spots. The only thing that had changed was her pictures. When she was little she used to have pictures of characters like Winnie-the-Pooh and Paddington Bear, but as soon as she was old enough to choose for herself, she'd swapped them for images of horses. Now she had a beautiful picture of a white palomino in a sunlit field, and a girl cantering a chestnut pony just like Honey along a gorgeous beach.

Clara couldn't imagine living anywhere else.

There was a gentle knock on her bedroom door and Mum came in with a plate of pancakes and some orange juice. Pancakes were Clara's favourite, but even the sight of them couldn't cheer her up. She turned over in bed, putting her back to Mum.

The bed moved as Mum sat down next to her. "I'm so sorry, darling," she said. "I know it feels horrible right now, but it is for the best, I promise."

Clara bit her lip so that she wouldn't cry again. "I want to see Honey," she said, her voice just a croak.

"OK," Mum said brightly, "we'll go down to the stables early so you can spend the morning with her before your lesson this afternoon. OK?"

"And I want to go to Pony Camp with Lisa," Clara added. Suddenly being away for six weeks seemed like a brilliant idea. She wouldn't have to be home while everything in her life got changed and rearranged.

"We'll have to see about that, love." Mum's sigh was so deep that the bed shook. "We're going to have to be a bit more careful with our money while we sort everything out. I'll have a look at it, but it might not be possible this year."

Clara buried her face in her pillow. Everything was going wrong.

Mum moved Clara's fringe off of her face and kissed her forehead. Clara squeezed her eyes tightly shut and felt a tear leak out.

"Eat your pancakes and get dressed, then we'll go and see Honey," Mum said softly.

As soon as Mum left, Clara started pulling on her riding clothes. She looked out of the window. Outside it was sunny and bright, but inside Clara felt grey.

U

"I'm going to go and talk to Sally, OK?" Mum said as they arrived at the stables. Clara nodded. "Love you," Mum called.

"Love you too," Clara replied quietly. She got out the car and crunched across the gravel into the yard. Even though she'd been here many times now, she still felt as excited as she had on the day she'd met Honey. As she passed Sally and Milly's house, Clara wondered if one of her new homes would be close to the stables. Thinking about moving made her tummy churn, and she twisted her fingers nervously in her hair.

Clara's feet took her automatically up to Honey's stall. Honey was standing with her head over the door. She whinnied in surprise when she saw Clara.

"Hi, Honey," Clara said delightedly. "I'm happy to see you too." She stroked Honey's nose and then felt the tears come again. Honey whickered in concern and nuzzled Clara with her heavy head.

"My parents are splitting up," Clara said, her voice wobbling. "And I've got to move house. Everything's changing and I don't know what to do."

Honey let Clara sob into her mane until all her tears were gone, then she looked at Clara with her wise, brown eyes, and gave her a nudge with her nose.

Clara knew that Honey was trying to tell her it would be OK. She wrapped her arms around Honey's strong neck and gave her a hug.

There was a gentle cough from behind her. Sally was standing there with a head collar and lead rein looped over her shoulder. She came over and stroked Honey's nose, then gave Clara a funny round brush.

"It helps if you brush while you talk," she said kindly. "Circular motions."

Clara brushed Honey's coat and Honey whickered in delight, making Clara smile.

"Your mum explained what's going on," Sally said. "Things will get better, I promise. Your mum and dad love you very much."

"No, they don't," Clara sniffled into Honey's mane. "Or they wouldn't be doing this."

"I know it's hard, but it will be OK." Sally put her arm around Clara and smiled, her brown eyes crinkling at the edges. For a second Clara realized how similar her deep brown eyes were to Honey's.

"Your mum had some errands to do,"

Sally continued. "I said you could stay here with me and spend some time with Honey before your lesson. I was just going to turn her out into the top field with her friends for a bit. Do you want to help?"

Clara wiped her eyes and nodded.

Sally put the head collar on Honey and Clara opened the stall door. Sally held on to the lead rein loosely as Honey trotted out. Honey clearly knew where she was going.

Sally and Clara led Honey up to the top field, making sure she didn't pull but walked neatly at Sally's shoulder. Sally opened the gate and two other horses, a little grey mare and an older bay mare, came over to greet Honey. "That's Apple," Sally told Clara, pointing at the grey, "and this one's Stormy."

Honey greeted the other horses happily, then started munching the fresh grass.

Clara suddenly thought about how

scared Honey had been at the last jumping lesson. She'd been so busy feeling sad about her family that she'd almost forgotten that Honey was upset too.

"Do you think she'll ever be able to jump?" she asked Sally. "I don't want her to be frightened or sad."

Sally looked over at Honey. As they watched, Honey dropped to her knees then lay on her back, rolling around on the grass.

"Does that look like a sad horse to you?" Sally said with a laugh.

"No," Clara said with a smile. Honey was rolling back and forth and rubbing her back like she was scratching an itch. She looked so happy!

"You're both having a bit of a tough time." Sally put her arm around Clara's shoulders. "But that adorable pony will be OK, and so will you. You'll get through it together."

4

As Clara walked back into the yard later that day, Lisa came hurtling towards her, kicking up stones and bits of gravel as she ran. "Well? Did you ask about Pony Camp?" she said eagerly. "I messaged you. Didn't you get it?"

Clara shook her head guiltily. She had got Lisa's messages; she just hadn't known what to reply. "I can't come," she said.

"What!" Lisa exclaimed. "I can't believe they said no!"

Clara fiddled with her hair.

"Now I have to go to camp on my own!" Lisa pouted.

Clara looked at her. "My parents are splitting up," she said, her voice wobbling a bit.

Lisa's face softened. "Oh no! That's rubbish," she said. "But why does it mean you can't come to camp?"

"I just can't, OK," Clara said.

Lisa pouted again and kicked the gravel.

"But we can have lots of fun for the rest of the holiday," Clara said comfortingly. She put her arm around Lisa. It felt odd that she was the one trying to cheer Lisa up, instead of the other way around. "Look," she said, pointing to the field, "Sally's setting up some jumps."

"OK," Lisa said grumpily.

"Come on, girls," Sally called, waving them over to where the horses were getting tacked up.

Clara rode Honey up to the field, Lisa following on Star. Sally and Mary, one of the other grooms, had positioned two sets of poles at the far end of the field. One set was lying flat on the ground, but the other was supported on big plastic blocks, making very low jumps, about the height of Clara's ankles.

"Right," Sally said once the rest of the class had arrived and the ponies had walked and trotted around for five minutes and were nicely warmed up. "We're going to split into two groups today. Lisa and Pari, Jasmine and Becca, you're going to be trying the jumps with Mary. Clara and Lena, you're with me and we're going to be doing floorwork for a bit longer."

Clara was feeling hopeful. Honey seemed happy and relaxed, her ears twitching eagerly and her tail hanging loosely.

But as soon as she saw the poles, Honey refused to follow the other horses to the end of the field.

"Come on, Honey, it's OK." Clara tried to reassure her. She clicked her tongue and nudged Honey with her heels, but Honey just stood still, refusing to move. Clara didn't know what to do. She sat helplessly as the other girls rode over to continue the lesson.

Sally spotted them sitting by the field gate and jogged over. "Poor Honey, you really don't like this, do you?" she murmured, stroking the pony's nose.

Sally took hold of Honey's reins and walked forward a few steps with her. "Try again," she said to Clara.

"Walk on," Clara said, and she tapped her heels on Honey's side.

Sally walked next to her and Clara patted her neck comfortingly, and finally they got Honey up to the end of the field. But even with Clara on her back encouraging her and Sally holding the reins steady, she still shied away from the poles, going around them instead of over them. Worst of all, every time Clara glanced at Lisa and Pari, she could see them laughing together.

By the end of the lesson, Clara and Honey had only gone over the poles once. Lisa and Pari were happily doing the jumps, trotting along together and laughing. Clara tried not to feel hurt. She got down off of Honey and ran her fingers through the pony's silky mane. Honey reached down and bumped her shoulder, as if she was saying sorry.

"It's OK, Honey." Clara kissed her nose.

"Don't worry," Sally said to Clara as she and Mary came over to help take the saddles off the horses. "Honey will get better. Something about jumping obviously scares her."

"Maybe you should learn to jump on a different horse?" Mary suggested.

"No!" Clara exclaimed. If she couldn't jump on Honey, she didn't want to jump at all. "Can I rub her down tonight?" she asked.

"Sure, if your mum doesn't mind you staying a bit longer," Sally told her. "It's been a pretty long day."

Clara thought about going home and her tummy turned topsy-turvy. She hoped Mum wouldn't mind her spending extra time with Honey.

As soon as the lesson was over, she ran over to the car park. Mum was waiting as usual. She rolled down the car window. "Can I stay a bit longer, Mum, please?" Clara asked.

"Of course," Mum said. "Are you doing something with the girls?" She turned to look across the car park at Lisa and Pari.

Clara glanced over. Lisa and Pari were jumping up and down excitedly as they spoke to Pari's mum. What was going on?

"No, I want to help with Honey," Clara said. "Sally says it's OK."

"Well, I need to go to the shops, so I'll do that and pick you up again in an hour," Mum said.

As Mum drove off, Clara walked back to the yard, past Lisa and Pari.

"Clara!" Lisa called. "Pari's coming to Pony Camp with me! Isn't that brilliant!"

Back in the yard, the horses were tied up in a line. Sally, Milly and Mary were looking after a pony each, rubbing them down with a grooming mitt.

"Oh, there you are. All OK?" Sally asked. Clara nodded. "Clara's going to help us out today," Sally continued. "Why don't you look after Honey with Milly?" she suggested, gesturing towards her daughter.

Clara nodded again. She still didn't trust

herself to speak. She couldn't believe Lisa was going to Pony Camp with Pari. It was so unfair! She bit her lip to stop the tears. She really didn't want to cry in front of everyone.

Milly was looking at her curiously, but she didn't say anything. "Grab a curry comb out of the grooming kit," she said in a kind voice.

Clara looked at the bucket at Milly's feet. There were lots of different brushes in there – a round plastic one, one that looked a bit like a broom... Clara picked out the one that looked most like a comb.

"That's a mane comb," Milly said. "Here." She picked out a round rubber brush and handed it to her. "This is the curry comb," she explained. "You use that first, going round in circles."

"Won't it hurt?" Clara asked, looking at the thick rubber.

Milly shook her head. "Horses have

strong skin. But only use it on her neck and back, not on her belly or her head."

Clara started to brush Honey in circles. She huffed happily and Clara felt happy too. She loved taking care of Honey.

"What next?" Clara said, once she'd brushed all over Honey's sides.

"Then we use the dandy brush to get rid of any mud and dirt," Milly said, giving her a brush that was a bit like a broom. She used the stiff bristles to brush Honey's coat and dust billowed out. Clara hadn't realized she was so dirty!

"Then use the body brush to make her coat nice and shiny." Milly held up a much softer brush.

"Make sure you brush in the direction the hair grows when you use the body brush," Sally added, coming over to show them. "You can brush her head with this one – very gently though."

Clara's arm was aching by the time she had finished using the smooth body brush, but it was worth it to look at Honey's gorgeous chestnut coat shining in the sunshine and to see her pony blink and huff with happiness. Then she and Milly watched as Sally went to each pony in turn, lifting up their feet so that she could carefully clean them with a hoof pick.

"You'd make a good groom, Clara," Sally said, as Clara gently combed Honey's mane. Clara felt a thrill of pride. She was so pleased that she stopped brushing – and Honey turned her head, giving a gentle huff as if she was saying, "Don't stop."

"I think Honey agrees!" Milly said with a giggle.

5

Beep! Beep! The car horn sounded outside the house. Clara ran down the stairs two at a time. Dad was coming to get her for her first-ever weekend at his new flat. Clara felt excited and nervous at the same time. Mum handed her a bag and gave her a kiss on her forehead. "Have a lovely time, darling," she said, pulling her in for a hug. "I've packed your riding things for your lesson on Saturday. Make sure Daddy knows what time you have to get there. You know how rubbish he is at remembering things like that!"

"I will," Clara said. She squeezed Mum tight, then opened the front door.

"See you on Sunday!" Mum said.

As Clara ran out to Dad's car, Mum waved at Dad and he waved back.

"Hello, darling," Dad said, reaching over to give her a massive hug. "I've missed you soooo much."

"Me too," Clara said, snuggling into him. Dad was wearing different clothes and he had a funny, scratchy beard, but at least his dad hug was the same.

"I've got lots of fun plans for us," Dad said. "Let's go and see the flat, then I thought we could go out for pizza. How's school? And Honey?"

As they drove, Clara told him all her news. Dad asked questions and made little *mmm-hmmm* noises. She couldn't remember the last time it had just been her and Dad, and it was really nice.

"Ta-dah!" Dad said as they pulled up into the driveway. "This is the new flat! What do you think?"

Clara looked up at the tall building and her hand went automatically to fiddle with her hair. It was a block of flats – as different from their lovely house as you could get.

"It's nicer on the inside," Dad said. He grabbed some shopping out of the car boot and they climbed the stairs to the flat.

Inside, everything was white and bare, like Dad hadn't moved in at all. The sofa was in one big room with the kitchen, and there was a TV on the wall.

"It's a bit different," Dad said, "but it's got everything I need. Including a special room for my special girl. This way!"

Dad led her down a corridor with three doors. "That's the bathroom, and my bedroom," he said, pointing to the doors as they passed, "and ..." he swung open the last door, "this one is yours."

This room wasn't white; it was bright pink. It had a duvet with pink horses on it and a pink furry rug. "What do you think?" Dad asked.

"Did you get all this ready for me?" Clara asked.

Dad nodded proudly. "Do you like it?"

"It's lovely!" she said, wrapping her arms around him. The rug was horrible, but Dad must have spent ages choosing it. She gave him a tight squeeze. At least the horse duvet wasn't too bad!

When Dad dropped her back home on Sunday night, Clara felt happy. They had had lots of fun, and he had been around all weekend, rather than spending time at work. They'd gone to the stables, and Dad had sat and watched while she had her lesson. Honey had still been scared of the poles, while Lisa and Pari were now doing little jumps and talking in loud voices about going to Pony Camp next week.

When she'd got off Honey, Dad had been there to help. "You know, you were really scared of ducks when you were little," he had told her.

"Was I?" Clara had giggled.

"Terrified! Every time anyone said 'quack', you'd cry!" Dad had said with a laugh. "I still don't know why!"

Somehow the silly story had made Clara feel better. She wasn't scared of ducks any more, and eventually Honey wouldn't be scared of jumping either.

When Mum opened the front door she gave Clara a massive hug. "I missed you!" she said. "How was it at Dad's?"

"Ummm," Clara replied, her fingers going to her hair.

Mum gave her a serious look. "It's OK if you had fun," she said. "In fact, it's brilliant. Dad and I both want you to be happy."

Clara felt her worry whoosh out of her in a big breath. "It was fun," she smiled. "But my bedroom is *very* pink!"

Mum laughed. "Well, I promise you can choose everything for your bedroom in our new house, OK?"

Clara grinned. Maybe having two homes wouldn't be so bad after all.

6

"And this is the small bedroom," the estate agent said. Clara felt her heart sink. It was horrible. Were they really going to have to leave their lovely house and live here? She glanced at Mum, but it looked as though she felt the same way Clara did.

Mum turned to Clara and put her thumbs down, blowing a raspberry. Clara giggled. "I don't think this is the one for us, do you, darling?" Mum said.

Clara shook her head.

"We'll keep looking," Mum told the estate agent.

Mum wound down the windows as they drove home and turned up the radio loud, singing along to a pop song and drumming her fingers on the steering wheel. It was a beautiful summer day, but Clara didn't feel summery at all. School had finished for the holidays yesterday, and Lisa had left for Pony Camp. She'd hugged Clara goodbye and promised to message her all the time, but Clara didn't really want to hear about all the fun Lisa was having. She still didn't know what she was going to do this summer.

As they drove past a field full of horses, Clara looked out at them, wondering what Honey was doing. She still needed to think of a way to make her realize that jumping could be fun...

"Do you want to go to the stables and visit Honey this afternoon?" Mum suggested.

"Can we?" Clara asked.

"Sure! Sally said you could drop by whenever you wanted." Mum grinned at her. "There's just one condition."

"What?" Clara asked.

"*Siiiing* with me!" Mum bellowed, turning the music up loud again.

Clara grinned and joined in with the song. They drove along, singing as loudly as they could.

When Mum dropped her at the stables, Clara went straight to Honey's stall. The door was open but Honey wasn't inside. Instead there was Milly, forking dirty straw into a wheelbarrow.

"Hello," Clara said in surprise.

"Oh, hi!" Milly turned to look at her. "Honey's turned out in the upper field. I was just mucking her out."

"Thanks," Clara replied. She turned to go

up to the field, but then she stopped. "Can I help?" she offered.

Milly smiled at her. "OK," she said, gesturing at a broom. "I've almost finished putting the old straw into the barrow. Now we brush the stall out and put fresh straw in."

Clara picked up the broom and started sweeping a corner of the stall, while Milly wheeled the old straw out. They worked in silence. Clara was surprised to find that she quite liked the sweeping. It was nice to think that she was making a cozy bed for Honey to sleep in.

"My parents are divorced too," Milly said suddenly.

Clara looked at her with surprise.

"Mum told me about your parents," Milly stammered. "I mean, she just said, in case you were feeling sad or anything."

Clara suddenly felt like she was going to

cry. She kept sweeping, stabbing the brush into the ground.

"Sorry," Milly said quietly. "It's just ... sometimes parents are happier when they don't live together."

Clara could feel the tears coming and she didn't want Milly to see them. "I'm going to see Honey," she said, throwing the brush down. She ran out of the stall without looking back.

Clara got all the way up to the top field before she burst into tears. Honey was there, standing under a tree with her friends Apple and Stormy. Clara climbed up on to the first rung of the fence. "Honey!" she called.

Honey saw her and trotted over, her ears flicking happily. "Hi, Honey," Clara said as her horse put her head over the fence to greet her. Honey huffed a hello, then nuzzled at her pocket for the Polos she knew would be there. Clara gave her one, then stroked her soft nose. "Oh, Honey," Clara said. "Why can't everything stay the same?"

Honey whinnied sympathetically.

Clara rested her head gently against Honey's and thought about what Milly had said. Dad and Mum *had* been happier over the past few weeks, now that they weren't arguing all the time. She just wished things didn't have to change. She wiped her eyes on the sleeve of her jumper.

"Do you think I should apologize to Milly?" she asked Honey.

Honey looked at her kindly, then blinked. Clara sighed. She gave Honey one last pat and climbed down from the fence.

Milly was sitting by the stalls, stroking the stable cat, when Clara arrived back in the yard. Clara went slowly up to her, twirling her hair around her finger. "I'm sorry," she said simply.

"It's OK," Milly said, with a big grin. "I'm sorry I upset you."

"It wasn't your fault," Clara said. "It's just … everything's so strange at the moment. We're moving house and I'll only see Dad every other weekend. And my best friend's gone to Pony Camp without me. This summer is going to be rubbish."

They both sat crosslegged on the floor and stroked the cat, who purred happily. "She likes it when you stroke her head like this," Milly explained, rubbing her fingers around the cat's ears.

Clara copied her and the cat purred in delight, nudging her head into Clara's hand. Clara smiled. "You know lots about animals, Milly," she said.

"That's because I live here," Milly said happily. "But we didn't always have the stables. Mum and my stepdad bought it when I was six." Milly gave her a side look, as if to check that Clara wouldn't be upset. "I love it here, but I wouldn't live here if my parents hadn't got divorced."

"Milly!" Sally was walking across the yard, leading Stormy behind her. Both girls scrambled to their feet. "Ah, there you are. Hello, Clara!" Sally said brightly. "Do you girls want to help get the ponies' dinners?"

Clara grinned. She'd never fed Honey before. "What do they have for dinner? Carrot stew?" she said, pulling a funny face. "Hay pancakes?"

Milly giggled. "Come on, I'll show you," she said.

They went into the feed room, the cat winding around their legs. It was a little room with a big whiteboard on one wall and lots of feed bins on the floor. There were different coloured buckets stacked up in the corner.

Clara watched as Milly measured out chaff and pony nuts into the buckets. On the whiteboard was a chart saying what each horse had to eat. "We don't feed them very much in the summer because they're out in the fields eating grass all day," she explained. "In winter they'll have a lot more."

By the time they had finished putting the right food in the right buckets, Sally had put all the ponies back in their stalls and was filling a net full of hay. Milly and Clara gave the horses their buckets and ran over to help.

"Do you mind doing all this?" Clara asked Milly.

Milly shook her head. "I love it. Mum's paying me to be a stable girl all summer and I can't wait. I want to work at a stables one day, so it's good practice. Besides, it's fun, isn't it?"

Clara nodded. She knew what Milly meant. It was hard work, but she loved being around the horses. Looking after them was almost as much fun as riding them.

"Maybe that's what you could do this summer!" Milly said brightly.

Before Clara could say a word, Milly began to explain to her mum about Clara not going to Pony Camp. "Clara could come and help here over the summer, couldn't she, Mum? You said she'd make a good groom!"

"She would!" Sally smiled. "And we always need help. If you come and do some chores with Milly and the others, I could take you both out riding. We could do some extra work on Honey's jumping."

"Do you mean it?" Clara asked. Her mind was racing. Spending the whole summer at the stables, seeing Honey every day *and* helping her with her jumping . . . it sounded perfect!

"It's hard work, looking after the horses," Sally said seriously, and then her face crumpled into a smile, "but we'll have lots of fun too. What do you think?"

Clara looked from Milly's eager face to Sally's kind one and flung her arms around them both.

"I think that's a yes, Mum," Milly giggled.

"Yes!" Clara squealed in excitement. "Yes, please!"

7

Clara got dressed carefully for her first day as a stable girl, wearing old jodhpurs and a T-shirt, and plaiting her long hair. Mum and Sally had spoken on the phone and arranged it all. Then Milly and Clara had chattered about the things they were going to do as stable girls together. It was going to be amazing!

When Mum dropped Clara off, Milly was waiting in the car park. "Hello, Clara!" she called. "Today's going to be so much fun!"

Their first job was mucking out the stalls while Sally turned the horses out into the fields. As they worked, Milly told Clara about when she'd got her horse, Apple. Then Clara told her all about seeing Honey for the first time.

"That was when I saw you riding Apple," Clara said shyly, "and I wished I could be as good a rider as you are."

"You already are!" Milly said. "You're definitely the best in your class. I heard Mum say you have a very good seat."

Clara felt her cheeks go warm at the compliment. Sally was always telling the girls in her class to sit properly. For a second she thought how amazing it would be to show off at the gymkhana, but then she remember about the jumping. "Honey doesn't like jumping," she told Milly. "She might not be able to do it."

"Yes, she will," Milly said firmly. And for some reason, Clara believed her. They spent the rest of the time chatting about horses and school and everything else that came into their heads. Clara was surprised when the stalls were all clean with a nice bed of straw in each one.

"Good job," Sally said approvingly as she came over with a tray of drinks and biscuits. "Now for your payment! I thought we could do your first extra lesson with Honey."

"Yes, please!" Clara grinned. She'd been so busy that she hadn't even said hello to her pony.

The girls sat down in a wheelbarrow and Sally explained what they were going to do. "I think Honey must have had a bad experience with her old owner," she said. "It's funny how much horses remember about the things that happen to them. One of the horses I used to look after, Sparkle, always got excited when she saw a red bucket, because her owners used to feed her from one!"

Clara and Milly laughed.

Once they'd finished their snacks, Sally led them up to Honey's field. "Honey!" Clara called. Honey trotted over, looking pleased to see her, as usual. Clara stroked her soft mane and Honey whickered happily.

Sally saddled Honey up while Milly laid out the poles. Clara held the reins and watched her horse closely. Every time she saw the poles, Honey's ears twitched warily. It was a bit like a horse version of the nervous way she twisted her hair!

Before she got on, Clara stroked Honey's nose and went on tiptoe to whisper in her ear. "There's nothing to be scared of," she murmured gently. "If you don't want to jump in the gymkhana, we won't do it, OK? We're a team, you and me."

Honey looked at her as if she understood every word, then she bent her head and nuzzled Clara's shoulder. Clara flung her arms around her huge head and hugged her back.

"Come on then," she said. "Let's give it a try."

"Ready?" Sally asked.

Clara nodded. She felt nervous, but determined to make Honey feel better. She didn't care if they had to try going over the poles a hundred times – she wasn't going to give up. Honey had made her feel better when *she* was upset, and Clara was determined to do the same!

"Good job!" Sally said as they put Honey back in her stall with a hay net. They'd gone over the poles so many times that Clara had lost count. Finally Honey had gone across them without flinching or shying away. They were a long way away from being able to jump, but it was a start.

Sally took a hosepipe and began rinsing down the yard. Clara stretched her arms. She felt hot and sticky and her shoulders ached from the riding and the grooming, but as she looked over at Honey in her stall, munching on the fresh hay, her coat gleaming, she felt a burst of happiness.

Honey looked up and her ears twitched happily too.

Just then a spray of water hit Clara. "Hey!" She turned around.

"Oops," Sally said, with a mischievous smile, and swung the hosepipe around towards Milly.

"Mum!" Milly squealed as the water hit her.

Clara giggled. The water actually felt nice and cool. She rubbed her face with her wet hand.

"You're not getting away with that, Mum!" Milly laughed. She ran off and came back seconds later with a bucket full of water and a sponge. "Clara, catch!"

But Clara was too slow and the sopping-wet sponge hit her in the tummy. "Argh!" she cried.

Milly burst out laughing.

"I'll get her for you, Clara!" Sally called. She turned the hosepipe towards Milly, the water arching up, drops shining rainbow colours in the sunshine.

Milly shrieked as the water splashed her. "Help!" she cried. "Clara, help!"

Clara picked up the wet sponge and threw it at Sally. It hit her in the shoulder with a squelch.

"Argh!" Sally cried. Suddenly she was chasing both girls with the hose. Clara and Milly grabbed the bucket and the sponge and ran, laughing and shrieking at the tops of their voices.

"Hide!" Milly gasped.

They ducked behind an open stable door, trying not to giggle. As they heard footsteps coming towards them, Clara counted quietly. "One, two, three, attack!" she whispered.

They leapt out from behind the door and threw the water over Sally…

Except it wasn't Sally!

"What's going on!" Clara's mum shrieked. She was drenched from head to toe, her hair plastered to her head and her top sticking to her body.

"Gotcha!" Sally came round the corner with the hose. "Oh, no! I'm so sorry, Mrs Walker!" she said, looking like she was trying not to laugh. "We were trying to cool off after a busy day!"

"Sorry, Mum! We thought you were Sally," Clara said.

Suddenly, as she looked at her mum standing in a puddle, Clara got the giggles.

Once she had started she couldn't stop. She caught Milly's eye and Milly burst out laughing too. The two of them laughed and laughed until Clara's belly ached. Then Mum began to giggle too, and Clara ran over and gave her a damp hug.

"Right, you two, go and get dry," Sally said. "Milly, can you lend Clara some clothes? Mrs Walker, you can borrow something of mine."

"Come on!" Milly led Clara into the house and up to her room. It was bright pink with pictures of horses all over the walls. In the middle was a familiar picture of a girl riding a pony on a beach.

"I have that same picture!" Clara gasped.

"It's my favourite!" Milly said.

"Mine too!" Clara grinned.

When they finally drove home later that afternoon, Mum and Clara were wearing matching Hollyhock Stables jumpers and leggings that they'd borrowed from Sally and Milly.

"I'm sorry about Pony Camp," Mum said, "but it seems like you're having a lot of fun at the stables."

"I am!" Clara said, and it was true. No matter what Lisa was doing at Pony Camp, it couldn't be better than this!

"Clara!" Mum called from downstairs. "Can you come down? There's something I want you to see!"

Clara put aside her summer project and stretched. Her teacher had told them to keep a diary during the holidays, and now she was a stable girl, Clara had loads of interesting things to write in it!

"Come and look at this," Mum called as Clara bounded down the stairs. On her computer screen were pictures of a house. It was smaller than their current one, but it had a pretty garden and a red front door with flowers all around it. "Auntie Maggi and I went to see it and it's lovely," Mum said, scrolling through the pictures. "There's one room in particular that you're going to love." She showed Clara a little room with a desk in it.

"An office?" Clara made a face.

"We'd make it into your bedroom, silly!" Mum said. "But, look, there's more..." She flicked to the next picture. "This is the view out of your window."

The picture showed the garden and, beyond, a field with three familiar ponies in it...

Clara turned to her mum, her mouth open wide. "Is that the stables?"

"Yes!" Mum grinned. "It's so close, you could see Honey every night if you wanted to – and when you get a bit older you'll be able to look after her all by yourself. What do you think?"

Clara flung her arms around Mum and squeezed her tight. "I love it!" she said.

"Me too," smiled Mum.

That night, Clara went to sleep to the sound of her mum singing to herself in the kitchen.

"That smell is making me hungry!" Milly groaned.

Clara and Milly were in Milly's kitchen, stirring a massive bowl full of grated apples, carrots, oats, oil and syrup.

"It's for the horses, not you!" Clara said with a giggle. Sally had asked if they wanted to make horsey treats today, and the girls had happily agreed.

"But it smells so good!" Milly said, pretending to lick the spoon.

"Don't!" Clara squealed. "You'll turn into a horse!"

"No, I won't—" Suddenly Milly stopped talking and grabbed her tummy. For a second, Clara thought that something was wrong – but then Milly dropped to her hands and knees and started making horse noises. "Neigh! Neeeeiiigh!"

Clara burst into giggles as she realized what her friend was doing. "Oh, help!" she cried. "My friend is a horse, whatever shall I do?"

She pretended to take a bite of the mixture too, then dropped to her knees. "Neigh!" she brayed. "Neeiiigh!"

Both girls rolled on the floor in fits of laughter.

"What's this, horses in the kitchen?" Sally said. The girls had been laughing so much they hadn't heard her come in. "There's so much noise in here that I'm guessing you must be finished with those horse treats."

"Almost!" Clara and Milly jumped up and began to stir the bowl again.

Once the mixture was ready, Sally put it into the oven to cook. "We don't let our horses have oats very often as it makes them over excited," she told the girls. "These are a real treat."

"We should have made human treats as well," Clara groaned.

Sally laughed. "I thought you might say that!" she said, and brought out two chocolate bars.

Milly and Clara grinned. "Thanks!"

"The oats will take a while to cook, and we need to make sure they're completely cool before we give them to the horses," Sally continued. "So why don't we give Honey another jumping lesson?"

"OK!" Clara agreed. Honey had made good progress over the last couple of weeks. She had got used to stepping over the poles.

Clara was delighted to see her becoming more confident.

Honey was in the top field with her pony friends. She whinnied as Clara ran up to the fence and trotted over to meet her. Clara helped Sally bring Honey into the indoor school and then, while Sally got Honey tacked up, Milly and Clara set up the poles on the ground as usual.

"I think she's ready to try a jump," Sally said.

"Really?" Clara gasped.

"Let's try it," Sally said. "If you want to jump in the gymkhana then we have to start practising."

Clara looked at Honey. She didn't seem nervous about the poles – in fact she was moving her hooves as if she was excited. "OK!" she squealed.

Soon Clara was up on Honey, looking at the course in front of her. Four poles were laid out on the ground, but the last one was further away and raised up on blocks to make a little jump. It was only as high as Clara's ankles, but it seemed as high as a mountain.

Clara could feel her heart thudding in her chest as she leant forward and made a clicking sound to Honey.

"Slowly now," Sally warned.

Clara trotted towards the poles. Honey didn't hesitate; she walked over one pole, then the next, then the next. Clara held her breath as they got to the jump. *Come on, Honey, you can do it!* she thought. *Jump!*

As if she'd heard her, Honey took a stride and then leapt over the pole in a slow half-hop. It didn't feel like the graceful flying jump that Clara had imagined – but it was a start!

She could see Milly doing a funny happy dance in the corner. Sally gave her a thumbs-up.

"Good girl!" Clara said, bending forwards to stroke Honey's mane. Honey huffed as if she was saying, "That was easy!"

"Right, let's do it again," Sally said.

Clara squeezed her right leg and pulled gently on the reins, taking Honey back towards the start of the course. Honey responded right away. She wasn't worried about jumping, in fact she seemed to be having fun!

Each time Honey stepped over the poles and did the little jump at the end, Clara felt her becoming more and more confident. She didn't know what was different this time – it was as if Honey had never been scared at all.

"She trusts you more," Sally said, her eyes twinkling. "You've spent so much time with her in the last few weeks. You've taken it slow and steady, and shown her that it's fun. You're a team."

"I guess so," Clara said. She got off Honey and patted her side. Not going to Pony Camp was the best thing that could have happened for her and Honey.

"One thing's for sure," Sally said. "Honey deserves one of your home-made horse treats!"

9

When Clara arrived at the stables the next day, Milly was sitting on the gate, waiting for her. As soon as the car pulled in to the car park, she jumped down and raced over. "Yay, you're here!" she said excitedly. "Mum's taking us on an adventure!"

"Where are we going?" Clara asked.

"I don't know!" Milly grinned. "But I think it's going to be a long hack because Mum's saddled up Stormy, Apple and Honey, and packed some sandwiches!"

As she looked at Milly, hopping from one foot to another, Clara started to feel excited too.

"Oh, yes, you'll be needing this." Clara's mum opened the car boot and gave her a lunchbox.

"You knew!" Clara squealed.

"Do you know where we're going?" Milly asked.

Mum just smiled mysteriously. "You'd better go and ask Sally," she said. She kissed Clara on the top of her head and got back into the car. "Have fun!"

Clara took the lunchbox, and she and Milly raced across the yard, gravel spraying out from under their feet as they ran.

Sally was standing by the stalls with Apple, Stormy and Honey. Honey huffed curiously as Clara went over to stroke her, as if she was asking what was going on.

"I don't know where we're going," Clara told her, reaching up to rub her on the nose. "But I think it's going to be fun!"

Sally put saddlebags over Stormy's broad

back and turned to look at the girls. "We're having the day off," she said with a smile. "No stable work today. Mary and the other grooms are looking after things here, while we go on an adventure!"

Clara and Milly grinned at each other in delight.

Sally helped them mount their horses and they started down the bridleway. Milly and Apple went first, then Clara and Honey, with Sally and Stormy behind them. Honey trotted happily, her ears twitching as she took in the sights and smells. The bridleway took them into the forest, and the sun shone down though the leaves, making pretty shadows on the ground. As Honey moved in a steady soothing rhythm underneath her, Clara couldn't stop grinning. Milly glanced back and Clara could see a smile on her friend's face too.

"Left or right?" Milly called out as they came to a turning.

"Right!" Sally yelled back.

"Where are we going, Mum?" Milly asked.

Sally rode past to take the lead. "You'll see!" she said, winking at Clara as she trotted by. Clara giggled. She couldn't wait to see where they were would end up!

As they came out of the forest, the track continued alongside a country road. A few cars drove past, but although Honey's ears flicked at the sound, she didn't seem scared. Clara patted her side reassuringly.

Soon they were walking downhill and the path beneath Honey's hooves became sandy. Clara's tummy flipped in excitement. At last she had an idea where they were going!

"We're here!" Sally called, trotting down the path and turning a corner.

Clara heard Milly's cry of delight as she followed. "Come on, Honey," she said.

They rode around the corner, and Clara's mouth stretched into a grin. They were at the beach!

"I can't believe we get to ride by the sea!" Milly gasped. "It's just like our picture!"

Clara looked around the beach, her eyes wide. She remembered coming here with Mum and Dad, but she never thought she'd be here with Honey! To the left was a busy stretch of sand, full of families. There were kids splashing in and out of the water, building sandcastles and shrieking. To the right there was a nature reserve sign, and Clara could see sand dunes, clumpy grass, and a few people walking dogs. It was much quieter on this side – and perfect for riding!

Milly was looking around too. "This is brilliant!" she said.

"All the ponies have been in the sea before," Sally said, "but let's take it slowly. There are a lot of different sights and sounds here. Some horses can be frightened of the water, so be aware of how your pony is feeling."

Clara reached forward to stroke Honey's neck. Her ears were forward – she didn't seem frightened; she seemed excited!

"Let's go!" Sally urged her horse forward and the girls followed behind.

"This is amazing!" Milly squealed.

"I know!" Clara replied.

The two girls and their ponies trotted side by side along the beach. Honey looked curious as her hooves sank deep into the sand, but Clara gave her a reassuring pat. When she said, "Walk on," Honey obeyed instantly.

Clara breathed in the fresh, salty air as they got closer to the water. Sally led

Stormy into the waves. Clara felt a thrill of excitement as she and Honey followed.

Honey hesitated as she got to the water. As a wave came in, she shied away. "It's OK. It's OK," Clara soothed, stroking her neck.

"You all right?" Sally called.

"Yes!" Clara yelled back. "Don't be a scaredy pony," she said gently to Honey. "Remember, you thought jumping was frightening, but that turned out to be fun. This will be the same!" She let Honey put her nose down to the water. Honey gave a deep huff, then trotted into the waves.

Clara grinned as Honey stepped into the water, the waves swishing in and out around her fetlocks. "Good girl!" she praised, and Honey's ears flicked in pride.

Sally and Stormy were walking along the beach in the shallow water, and Clara turned Honey to follow them. She could see the shadow of her and Honey on the sand, looking like a perfect horse and rider from a photograph.

"Now, let's canter!" called Sally.

Clara let Honey speed up. Suddenly they were racing along the sand, Clara's hair streaming out like Honey's mane and tail, water splashing up behind them.

"Wahooo!" Clara yelled out loud. She finally knew how the girl in her picture felt – and it was amazing!

After a while, Sally slowed the pace and took them back on to the beach. "Let's stop here for a bit and have our sandwiches," she called.

She got off of Stormy, then helped the girls down.

"Can we go for a paddle, Mum?" Milly asked.

"Of course," Sally grinned.

While Sally gave each horse some water and a carrot, Clara and Milly took off their shoes and rolled up their leggings. The sand felt silky and smooth between Clara's toes. She grabbed Milly's hand and they ran, squealing, into the water. "It's cold!" Clara shrieked.

"No water fight this time!" Milly joked.

Once they'd eaten their lunch, they got back on to their ponies and returned along the beach the way they'd come. Honey wasn't nervous about the waves any more. She seemed to enjoy the water splashing all around her.

Eventually they could see the pathway in the distance. Clara felt sad for a moment, but then she urged Honey forward for one last canter and whooped with joy.

As they got back to the path, Clara spotted someone waving. Mum was standing by her car with her camera looped around her neck!

"Did you see us in the sea?" asked Clara happily.

"It looked great out there!" she said. "I got some brilliant pictures." She took the empty saddlebags from Sally and put them in the car. "I'll meet you back at the stables," she said. "Enjoy the ride home!"

Everyone was quiet but happy as they rode back to the stables. "That was one of the best days of my whole life!" Clara told Sally as they got off their horses. Without thinking about it, she threw her arms around the stable owner, giving her a big hug. Sally smiled down at her.

"Me too!" Milly said. "I'm never going to forget it!"

"And we have photos of us riding in the sea!" Clara added.

As Clara reached up and stroked Honey's white blaze, Honey nuzzled her head into her shoulder. Clara had had a brilliant day – and Honey had too!

10

"Bye, Dad!" Clara yelled as she shut the car door and ran up to Mum's house. "Hi, Mum!"

"Hello, darling," Mum said as she opened the door. Dad beeped the horn and Clara waved at him. Mum waved too.

But suddenly Clara flew back out of the door and towards the car. "Dad! Don't forget about the gymkhana! It's on Saturday at three o'clock."

"I'll be there," Dad said. "It's on the calendar!"

Clara grinned. Dad had bought a special calendar with pictures of horses on it so he could write down all her riding lessons and their weekends together. Clara was getting used to going between Mum's house and Dad's flat. Sometimes it was annoying, like when she left a book or some clothes that she wanted at the wrong house, but mainly it was working out fine. She and Dad went bowling and bike riding together, and with Mum she watched films and had Saturday-night ice cream. And whether she was at Dad's or Mum's, she still went to see Honey every day.

"Lisa called for you," Mum said as they went inside. "She's back from Pony Camp and she wants to meet you at the stables before your lesson."

"Oh!" Clara exclaimed. Six weeks had gone by really fast and she'd barely thought about her best friend. In fact, she wasn't even sure if Lisa *was* her best friend any more.

"You'd better go and see her," Mum said. "And if she tries to boast about Pony Camp, you have lots of exciting pony news to tell her too!"

"And then we had a campfire and we all cooked marshmallows on sticks!" Lisa said as she and Clara walked up to the yard. "It was the best thing ever!"

"It sounds great!" Clara said. It was really nice to see her friend. Lisa had given her a big hug – and a present too: a special badge from the camp with a picture of a jumping horse on it, with a matching one to put on Honey's bridle.

"I missed Star so much!" Lisa said as they got to the stalls.

"I had a brilliant time at Pony Camp," came a voice from the barn, "but Lisa hated it. She cried *every* night."

It was Pari! Clara glanced at Lisa, who was frozen to the spot.

"Every time we did anything she cried," Pari's voice continued. "She didn't like her pony, or the food, or any of the activities. Everyone called her Baby Lisa because she spent so much crying."

Lisa's face turned pink and she ran out of the yard. "Lisa, wait!" Clara called after her.

She was beginning to chase after her when Milly came out of her house. "Hi, Milly!" Clara said breathlessly. "Can you help me find Lisa?"

"Is she back?" Milly made a face.

"She's nice really, and she's upset. She had a horrible time at Pony Camp." Clara quickly told Milly what had happened.

"OK," Milly nodded. "Let's look for her."

Milly went up to check the fields, while Clara ran to Star's stall. She was sure Lisa would be there, but there was no sign of her.

"Have *you* seen Lisa?" Clara asked the bay mare, but Star just took another bite of hay from her net.

Clara was about to turn away, when she heard a noise from behind the door. She peered over it, into the stall, and a tearful face stared back up at her.

Lisa was huddled against the inside of the door, sitting on an upside-down bucket.

Clara opened the door and stepped inside. She thought for a moment then picked up a curry comb and handed it to her friend. "It helps if you brush while you talk," she said, smiling.

Lisa took the brush and began to gently groom Star with it. "I hated camp," she sniffed. "I wanted to come home straight away. Everyone was horrible. I'm so sorry

I was mean to you," she said with another sob. "And I'm really sorry about your parents. I ... I didn't know what to say when you told me."

"It's OK," Clara said, and realized to her surprise, that it was. Despite everything, she'd had the best summer ever.

"Thank you for coming to find me," said Lisa, wiping the tears away from her eyes and giving a small smile.

Clara opened the stall door. "Come on," she said, "I want to show you what Honey and I have been doing this summer!"

Milly was in the yard when Clara stepped out of the stall. "Did you find Lisa?" she called. "Oh," she added shyly as Lisa appeared behind Clara. "Hi."

"This is my best friend, Lisa," Clara said to Milly. "And this is my *other* best friend, Milly," she said to Lisa.

Milly gave a huge grin. For a second Lisa

looked confused, but then she smiled too. "Hi, Milly," she said.

Clara grabbed both her friends by the hands. "I was just about to tell Lisa about Honey's jumping!" she said.

"Honey can jump now?" Lisa asked excitedly.

"She's brilliant!" Milly told her.

"Come on!" Clara squealed, and pulled her friends across the yard to find Honey.

U

On the day of the gymkhana, Clara woke up with butterflies in her tummy. She pulled her riding clothes on, brushed her fringe and tied her long brown hair into a neat plait. Then she ran downstairs, dodging around all the boxes. She and Mum had packed all their things, and would be moving to their new home tomorrow. Clara was sad about leaving her old house, but excited about finally being in her new bedroom, where she could see the stables from the window. She and Mum had picked out a lovely paint colour for her new room: a bright yellow that reminded Clara of sunshine.

Mum had printed all the photos from the ride at the beach and framed a big one of Clara and Honey galloping. Best of all, Mum said that Milly and Lisa could come round for a sleepover as soon as they had settled in. Clara was happy that Milly and Lisa had made friends so quickly. Lisa had been much kinder since she'd got back from Pony Camp. Now, when she accidentally said something a bit mean, Milly copied her in a funny voice, and soon all three girls were laughing together.

"Let's go!" Mum called. "Honey will be waiting!"

Clara patted her pocket to make sure that she had some Polos. If everything went well today, Honey would deserve them!

At the stables, there were lots of people, chattering loudly with excitement. There was colourful bunting draped over the gate, and the yard was clean and tidy. All the horses looked gorgeous, as they poked their heads out of the stalls. Everyone had spent ages grooming their horses and ponies the previous day, and Clara had even plaited Honey's mane and tail.

Clara took Mum up to Honey's stall, hoping that her pony still looked as smart as she had the day before. As they got close, Honey stuck her head over the door and gave a happy neigh.

"Hello to you too!" Clara said, reaching up to stroke Honey's nose.

"Oh, she looks *adorable*!" Mum exclaimed as she saw Honey's beautiful mane.

"Hi!" Lisa said as she rushed over. "Are you ready? I want to get the best seat!"

Clara grinned. Her best friend hadn't changed *that* much. But for once she agreed. Her class wasn't doing their jumping display until three o'clock, but Lisa and Clara had decided to get there early so that they could watch all the other classes. There was someone special that they had to cheer for – Milly!

Lisa and Clara clapped as loudly as they could when Milly and Apple trotted out into the field. Milly's course was much more complicated than the one that Clara and Lisa would be doing. It had full-size jumps and even a white five-bar gate to leap. But Milly and Apple made it look easy!

The girls cheered and yelled, and Milly

gave them a happy wave as she and Apple left the field.

"Right, you girls had better go and get ready," Mum said. "I'll see you in the barn." Their display was going to be in the indoor school, where they'd had their first lesson all those weeks ago.

Clara twisted the end of her plait nervously, but when she realized what she was doing, she stopped. She knew Honey could do it. "Good luck!" Mum said, giving her a kiss on her forehead.

Clara and Lisa went round to the yard, where Sally and Mary were getting the horses ready.

"I'm scared," Lisa said quietly. "I didn't practise jumping at Pony Camp."

"Don't worry," Clara said, giving her friend's hand a squeeze. "We're going to be doing loads more jumping next term. Today is just meant to be fun!"

"OK!" Lisa smiled and ran over to Star.

"You think jumping is fun now, don't you?" Clara said as she went up to Honey. Honey whickered happily and nuzzled her head into Clara's side. Clara laughed and kissed the top of her nose. "Come on, Honey, let's show everyone what we can do!"

"Next up, our beginners' jumping display," Sally announced to the crowd. Clara looked over and spotted Milly, doing her excited dance at the edge of the barn. Her eyes scanned the seats anxiously. Where was Mum?

Honey huffed and shook her head, and Clara realized she was gripping the reins too tight. "Sorry, Honey," she said. "I'm not worried about the jumping. I just need to find Mum..." Her voice trailed off as she spotted someone waving from the back row. It was Mum, and next to her, waving wildly, was Dad!

Clara gave a gasp and Honey tossed her head again. Clara patted her side reassuringly. She had to concentrate, for Honey's sake. She gave a tiny wave to Mum and Dad, and then turned to listen to Sally.

"First up, Lisa and Star!"

Clara gave her friend a smile as she trotted into the arena.

As Lisa and Star hadn't practised all summer, the jumps were set the lowest they could go, the same as they had been before Lisa went to camp. But Lisa and Star did them well and the audience clapped loudly. Lisa's face was flushed and happy as she took her rosette from Sally.

Pari and Misty did the jumps at the same level, and also got a round of applause.

The rest of the class had their jumps

slightly higher. All the audience clapped and cheered as, one by one, the horses and riders leapt over the jumps, turned to complete the circuit.

"Lastly, Clara and Honey," Sally called out. "These two have both had a difficult summer, but they've worked together and overcome a lot. Just a few months ago, Honey was so afraid to jump that she wouldn't even go near the poles. But with a lot of kindness and patience from Clara, they've made a huge improvement." As she spoke, the stable hands set the jumps to the highest level yet. There was a murmur from the audience. Sally turned and gave them a thumbs-up.

Over in the corner, Clara spotted Milly standing with Lisa and Star. Both girls waved excitedly.

"Come on, Honey, it's you and me," Clara said. She sat up in the saddle and urged her pony forward. Honey trotted on happily. They did one circuit of the arena, then Clara lined Honey up in front of the jumps. *Come on, Honey, you can do it!* she thought as she tapped Honey's sides with her feet. Honey raced up to the first jump and cleared it with one big bound. She cantered to the next one and cleared that too. Clara could hear the audience cheering as they leapt over one jump then another. It was like flying!

As Honey cleared the last jump and finished the course, Clara couldn't stop grinning.

"A brilliant round for Clara and Honey!" Sally announced, handing Clara something brightly coloured – her first-ever rosette! "Well done!" Sally smiled. "I knew you could do it!"

Clara slid off of Honey and flung her arms around Sally's neck. "Thank you!" she said happily.

As Clara and Sally led Honey to the side of the school, Mum, Dad, Lisa and Milly all rushed over. "You came!" Clara grinned at Dad.

"You were brilliant!" Dad said, scooping her up and swinging her around.

"I'm so proud of you," Mum said, giving her a big squeeze.

Honey gave a whicker and Sally stroked her nose. "Yes, we're proud of you too!" Sally said. "It's been a good summer, hasn't it?"

"It's been so brilliant." Clara stroked the white blaze on Honey's nose. "I'm going to be sad when I'm back at school and not here every day."

"Well, you can come as much as you like. And there's always the holidays," Sally said. "Maybe you could be a stable girl again at Christmas?"

Clara looked at Milly and grinned with excitement. "Yes, please!"

Sally looked at Lisa and her smile widened. "Would you like to help out as well, Lisa?" she asked. "I can give you and Star some extra jumping lessons?"

Lisa's face broke into an enormous smile. "Yes! Thank you!" she gasped.

Milly, Clara and Lisa grabbed hands and jumped up and down. Clara couldn't wait for Christmas at Hollyhock Stables!

"Right, you three," Mum said, "see to the horses, and then I'll take you all for an ice cream."

"Not a secret ice cream then?" Dad laughed.

"Not this time," Mum replied with a grin.

"Are your parents getting back together?" Lisa whispered as the three girls walked the horses across the yard.

Clara looked back at where her mum and dad were chatting and shook her head. "No," she said, "but I think that's OK."

Honey whickered in agreement. Clara laughed and led her back to her stall.

"First I'm going to give you a nice rub down," she promised Honey. "Then, my brave, adorable pony, you can have all the Polos you can eat!"

Pony
Care Tips!

Grooming!

Grooming is very important when a horse has been for a ride – it makes them nice and clean, and best of all, you get to spend some time giving them lots of love and attention. You should always have help from an experienced adult, and never stand directly behind a horse in case it kicks.

1: Tie your horse's lead rope to a post in a quick-release knot, or ask a friend to hold them steady.

2: An adult should clean your horse's feet with a hoof pick, carefully taking out all the stones and dirt. The middle part of the hoof is called the "frog"! The frog is soft and squishy, and much more sensitive than the rest of the hoof, so don't use the hoof pick in that area.

3: Use a curry comb. Move the brush in small circular motions over the horse's body, but avoid bony areas like the face, spine and legs.

4: Use a dandy brush. Use the brush in short, straight flicking motions to whisk the dirt out. Do not use on the horse's face, ears, mane, tail, legs, or any clipped area.

5: Use a body brush. The body brush can be used all over the horse to make its coat lovely and shiny. Brush gently around the face though!

6: Brush out the mane and tail. Use a mane comb or even your fingers to separate any tangly bits, then gently comb it though. When brushing the tail, always stand to the side of the horse so there's no chance of getting kicked! You could even plait your horse's mane or tail to make them look extra special.

Mucking out!

Clara learns lots of skills when she works at Hollyhock Stables. Here's what she learnt about cleaning out a horse's stall.

You will need:

- A wheelbarrow
- A pitchfork or spade
- Some clean straw
- A messy horse stall!

1: Take out the horse's hay net and water bucket.

2: Use a pitchfork or a spade to put the manure and wet or dirty straw into a wheelbarrow.

3: Shovel the clean, dry straw to the sides of the stall to use later.

4: Sweep the floor and shovel up any remaining dirty, wet bedding into the wheelbarrow.

5: Leave the floor to dry completely.

6: Use a pitchfork to spread the clean straw from the sides of the room across the floor, adding a top layer of fresh straw.

7: Replace the horse's water and feed.

Now you have a cosy bed for your happy horse!

Spot the Pony!

Honey has a beautiful chestnut coat, but horses and ponies come in all kinds of colours. Use our horse colour guide below to see how many different types you can spot!

Appaloosa

Appaloosa horses have white patches on their backs with spots on. Some people say it looks like they have blankets on their backs!

Bay

Bay horses have brown bodies with black manes and tails. They often have black patches on their legs, faces and ears.

Black

Black horses are very rare. True black horses have black manes and tails and coats with no brown hairs in at all.

Chestnut

Chestnut horses like Honey have red coats. Light chestnut horses are called "sorrel" coloured and dark chestnut horses are called "liver" coloured.

Grey

Grey horses are often born another colour and turn grey as they get older. Their coats and manes are grey.

Palomino

Palomino horses have golden coats and white manes and tails.

Pinto

Pinto horses look like they've been splashed with paint. They have much bigger splotches than the spots of an Appaloosa. Some Pintos are white with coloured splotches, and others are coloured with white splotches.